STAR WARS®

REY MEETS BB-8

WRITTEN BY **ELIZABETH SCHAEFER**

ILLUSTRATED BY **BRIAN ROOD**

Printed in the United States of America

First Edition, December 2015

1 3 5 7 9 10 8 6 4 2

Library of Congress Control Number on file

FAC-029261-15306

ISBN 978-1-4847-0480-6

ISBN 978-1-4847-5342-2

Visit the official *Star Wars* website at: www.starwars.com.

This is Rey.

Rey lives on a planet called Jakku.

Jakku is hot and sandy.

A big battle was fought there
a long time ago.

On Jakku, Rey explores
the old ships.

She looks for broken things.

Then she fixes them.

Every day, Rey trades the things
she finds for food.

She trades with an alien
named Unkar.

Unkar is not always fair.

Rey takes the food back to her home.

She does not have a family.

Rey is alone.

One night, Rey was eating dinner.

She heard a beeping noise.

It sounded like a droid.

The droid sounded scared.

Rey ran toward the noise.

She found a mean alien.

The alien had trapped
a little droid in a net.

The droid beeped at the alien.

The droid wanted to escape!

Rey told the alien to stop.

She did not want the droid
to get hurt.

The alien did not want to fight Rey.

He left her and the droid alone.

Rey took the net off the droid.

The droid said his name was BB-8.

"What are you doing here?"
Rey asked.

BB-8 wouldn't tell her.

He said it was a secret.

Now that BB-8 was safe,
Rey tried to go home.

But BB-8 did not want her to leave.

BB-8 did not want to be alone.

Rey agreed to take BB-8 with her.

But she said BB-8 could stay for only one night.

The next morning,
Rey took BB-8 into town.

She wanted to trade with Unkar
for more food.

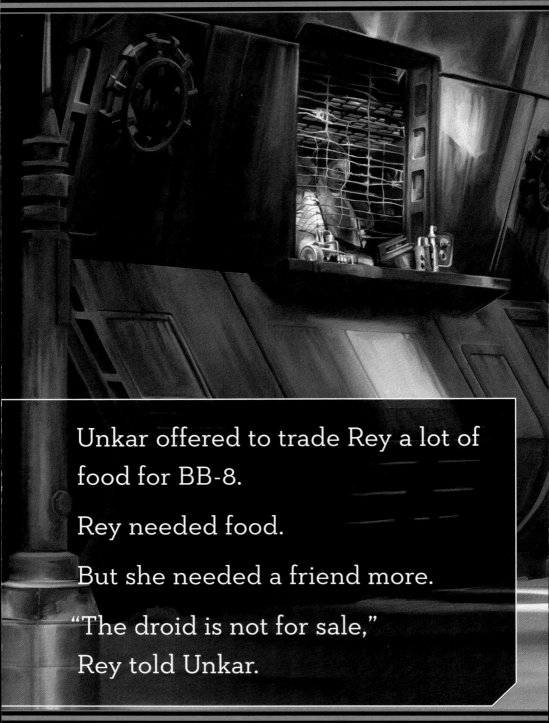

Unkar offered to trade Rey a lot of food for BB-8.

Rey needed food.

But she needed a friend more.

"The droid is not for sale,"
Rey told Unkar.

Unkar was very angry.

But Rey did not care.

Rey is not alone anymore.

BB-8 is not alone anymore.

Now Rey and BB-8 have each other.